For Gretchen, who shared the journey,
heard the words and made it happen.

L.J.

For my family, who show me every day
what it means to be supportive.

N.D.

A spider, small and dainty, got all ready for a bath.

Her mother wove a web and made a sturdy, silken path.

The mother said, "The water's fine I won't be far away."

The little spider hugged herself and heard somebody say:

"There's a spider in the shower, I will NOT be getting in.

It will catch me in the net it's taken half its life to spin.

It'll twirl me like a dancer in a bubbled-up ballet.

I may look a little dirty, but that's how I'm gonna stay!"

Then Mommy said, "Now Tillie, there's no spider anywhere.

It's just your imagination weaving stories in the air.

Would you like the water hotter?

Would you like it cool instead?

Won't you please take off your slippers?"

Tillie sighed and shook her head.

"There's a spider I am certain, and he's hairy and he's old.

With a motorcycle jacket, and a tooth made out of gold.

With a patch across one eye, and a hand that has a hook.

Twigs have muddied up my hair but I kinda like the look."

Mommy said, "You silly Tillie, there is nothing in the tub,

except your rubber ducky, and a sponge so you can scrub.

Here's some shampoo for your tangles,

soap and water for the dirt,

hurry up, we're having pizza,

and there's ice cream for dessert."

Tillie stood there bravely brambled,

with the pine pitch on her nose,

made a sad face in the mirror, made a pile of all her clothes,

scattered leaves onto the carpet,

dusted daylight from her skin

and her voice said in a quiver, "Step aside, I'm coming in."

Now she barely heard the shrieking

and she hardly heard the yelp,

or the startled voice that shouted

"Mama, save me! Mama, HELP!

There's a girl inside my tubby

and she's hideous and weird

with the woods inside her hair

and a sudsy, foamy beard."

Tillie peeked between her fingers,

water misting on her skin,

in between the spray and spatter,

she blinked once, then blinked again.

For there, huddled in the corner

near the tiles of ocean blue,

was a teeny tiny spider

with a towel and shampoo.

Spider clutched the towel tighter,

made a face and balled her fist,

threw a squishy, soggy slipper...

but, alas, the slipper missed.

Tillie hid behind the curtain, Rubber Ducky hid there too,

heard a "splat" that made them giggle

from the slipper spider threw.

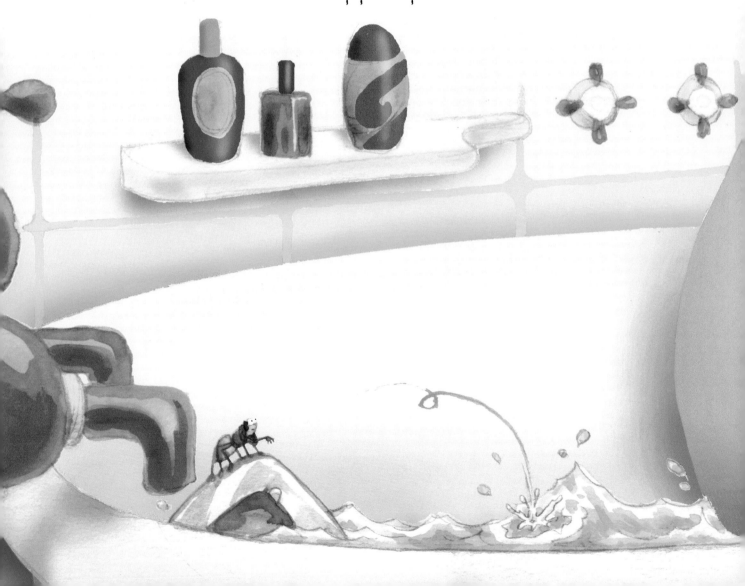

That's when Tillie waved a little,

Spider paused, then did the same.

Then they winked at one another, it was like a silly game.

Spider danced around on eight feet,

Tillie hopped around on two,

and they got a little dizzy from the bubbles that they blew.

Tillie's mother heard the ruckus,

every splash and laugh and shout,

and she couldn't help but wonder

what the noise was all about.

"Mommy, listen, can you hear me?

There's a web up on the wall

with a bunny-slippered spider and she's really, really small.

And at first I think I scared her, but now I make her smile.

Put my ice cream in the freezer, I'll be in here for a while."

CPSIA information can be obtained
at www.ICGtesting.com
Printed in the USA
LVIC06n1927171017
552803LV00005B/17